S0-AAC-084

By Francine Prose · Illustrated by Einav Aviram

LEOPOLD, the LIAR of LEIPZIG

JOANNA COTLER BOOKS
An Imprint of HarperCollinsPublishers

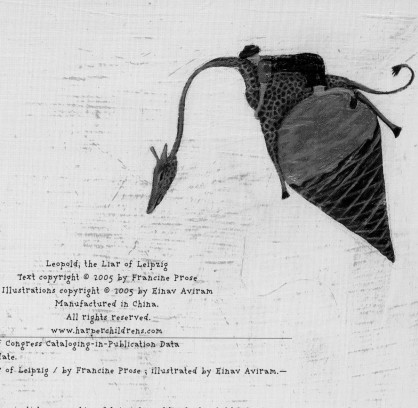

Leopold, the Liar of Leipzig
Text copyright © 2005 by Francine Prose
Illustrations copyright © 2005 by Einav Aviram
Manufactured in China.
All rights reserved.
www.harperchildrens.com

Library of Congress Cataloging-in-Publication Data
Prose, Francine, date.
Leopold, the liar of Leipzig / by Francine Prose ; illustrated by Einav Aviram.—
1st ed.
p. cm.
Summary: After a scientist accuses him of lying, Leopold, who has told tales in
Leipzig's zoo for many years, is surprised to find that he must explain the nature
of storytelling.
ISBN 0-06-008075-2 — ISBN 0-06-008076-0 (lib. bdg.)
[1. Storytelling—Fiction. 2. Zoos—Fiction. 3. Zoo animals—Fiction. 4. Leipzig
(Germany)—Fiction. 5. Germany—Fiction.] I. Aviram, Einav, ill. II. Title.
PZ7.P94347Le 2005   2003015417
[E]—dc22

Typography by Alicia Mikles
1 2 3 4 5 6 7 8 9 10
❖
First Edition

To Marisa, Forrest and Theo
—F.P.

For my parents,
Ryna and Moshe

And thank you to Joanna, Justin
and their crew for helping
turn a green dream into a
multicolored reality
—E.A.

Every Sunday afternoon the people
of Leipzig would gather in the city's
magnificent zoo, and Leopold would
tell tales of faraway places.

"In the land of Lusitana all the ladies look like lizards and the lizards all look like ladies."

"What kind of ladies?" asked Leopold's listeners.

"Lovely ladies," said Leopold.

"In the country of Carthaginia cats catch caterpillars and cook them in casseroles in costly cafés."

"Cooked caterpillars?" cried the crowd.

"It's a delicacy," said Leopold.

"The great galaxy of Gelato
is governed by a gabby gorilla named Gertrude."

"A gorilla governor?" gasped the group.

"Gabby Gertrude," said Leopold.

And so it went, Sunday after Sunday, year after year. The children who loved Leopold got older and brought their children to hear Leopold's tales.

Then one chilly winter day
a famous scientist and explorer,
Doctor Doctor Professor Morgenfresser,
arrived in Leipzig to give a lecture
in the great Town Hall.

DOCTOR DOCTOR
PROFESSOR
10AM
FREE
ADMISSION
TOWN HALL
MORGENFRESSER

Every seat was filled as the Professor began:

"In China people wear robes and eat noodles."

"In Egypt there are giant pyramids."

"In Antarctica black-and-white penguins are the only creatures in the landscape."

One by one, the audience left, except for those who had already fallen asleep.

"Why was no one interested in my adventures?"
asked Doctor Doctor Professor Morgenfresser.
  A young boy spoke up. "Because they were all so
boring compared to Leopold's!"

Once Doctor Doctor Professor Morgenfresser was told about the places in Leopold's stories, he became very angry and cried,

"YOUR LEOPOLD IS A LIAR! ARREST HIM!"

Poor Leopold! He was taken off to jail before he could say a single word in his own defense. Now it was his turn to feel like one of the animals in the zoo, without anyone to tell him stories.

A week passed, then another. Finally, Leopold was taken before twelve of the harshest and fiercest judges in Leipzig.

At the trial the greatest scholars in Europe proved there was no land of Lusitana, no country of Carthaginia,

and certainly no galaxy of Gelato.

And a woman who had grown up in the
house next door to Leopold swore that he
had never traveled anywhere—until he
came to Leipzig.
Things looked bad for Leopold.

Slowly he turned and faced the court. "Clearly I'm innocent."

"But you lied about everything!" the judges scoffed.

"Don't you see? You can make up all sorts of fantastic things, and unless you say that it actually happened, or that you actually saw something—it's only a STORY.

I'm not Leopold the Liar!"

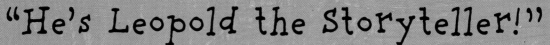

"He's Leopold the Storyteller!"
the people cried.
    "Case dismissed!"
pronounced the judges.

And so disappointed Doctor Doctor Professor
Morgenfresser went off on his travels, and that very
Sunday afternoon, Leopold returned to his spot at the zoo.

"In the province of Petunia," said Leopold, "parading piglets play the pipes at parties for puppies." "What kind of parties?" "Birthday parties," Leopold said. "Perfectly pleasant parties."

And the people of Leipzig gathered close to listen to Leopold the Storyteller's marvelous tales.

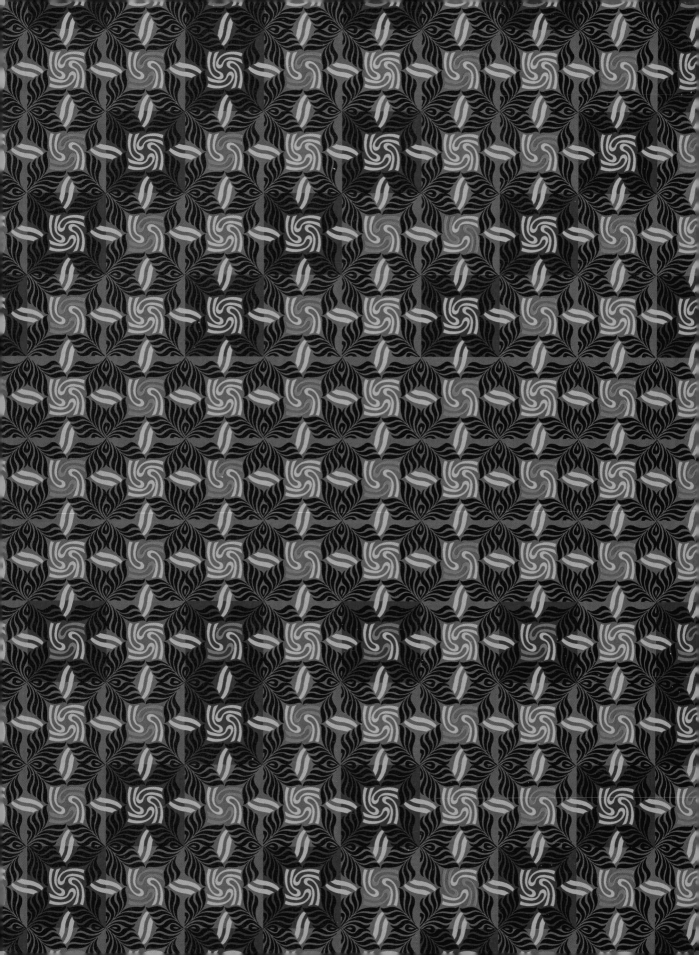